To Jack, Feli and Etta — M.M.

For Neil and Tiff — G.A.

EGMONT
We bring stories to life

First published in Great Britain 2017 by Egmont UK Limited
The Yellow Building, 1 Nicholas Road, London W11 4AN

www.egmont.co.uk

Text copyright © Matthew Morgan 2017
Illustrations copyright © Gabriel Alborozo 2017

The moral rights of the author and illustrator have been asserted.

ISBN 978 1 4052 8297 0

A CIP catalogue record for this title is available from the British Library.

THANK GOODNESS FOR BOB

Matthew Morgan   Illustrated by Gabriel Alborozo

EGMONT

Max worried. A lot.

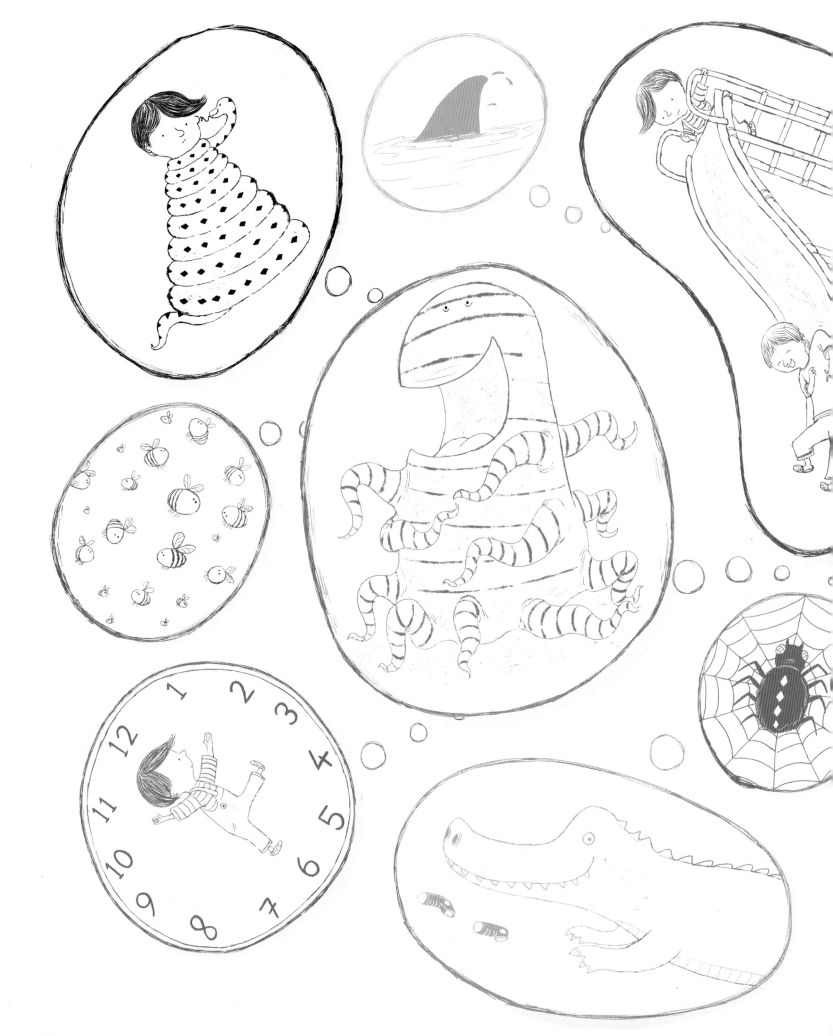

Unlike his dog, Bob,
who didn't worry at all.

Max worried that **no one liked him** . . .

and that some people **liked him too much**.

He worried that he might be
wearing **too many clothes** . . .

and that he might
not be wearing enough.

Max worried about being bitten by **spiders**,

abducted by **aliens**

and mauled by **monsters**.

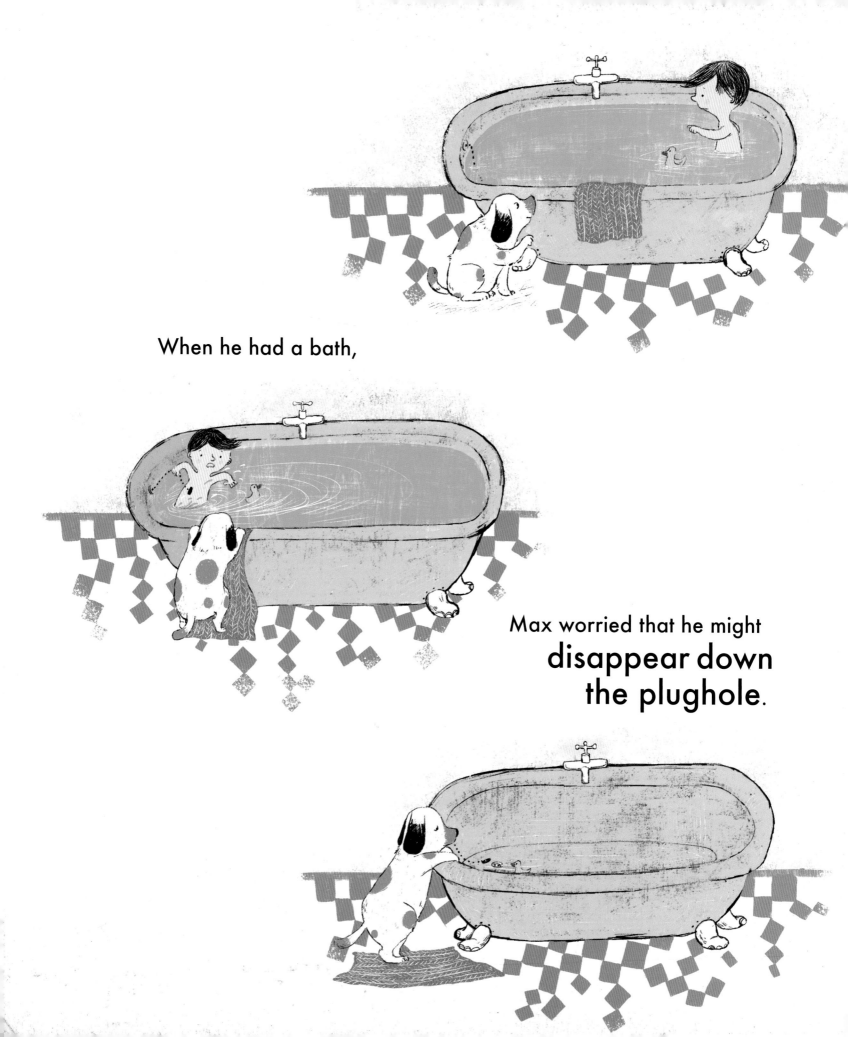

When he had a bath,

Max worried that he might
**disappear down
the plughole.**

And when he lay in bed he worried
that someone — or something —
**was lurking in
the shadows.**

Max had so many worries that they filled his head, making him feel **dizzy** and **numb**.

But Max didn't dare tell anyone about them.
He thought his parents would be **too busy**,

his sister would **tease him**

and his teacher would think he was a **fool**.

But everyone knew.

Everyone knew, but none of them knew what to do,
because Max's worrying just made them worry too.

It was as if the worries in Max's head were spreading.
Before long they would **take over the world!**

Thank goodness for Bob.

Bob didn't worry. Bob took life in his stride.

And he knew just what to do.
"Let's talk," Bob said.

So Max **talked** and Bob **listened**.

And as Max talked, the worries bubbled out of his head and floated around the room.

A room full of bubbles, a worry in each one.

Out in the open, Max's worries seemed very different.

Some of them looked small.

Some of them looked *silly*.

Bob reached out a paw. **Pop!**
A worry disappeared.

Bob kicked a bubble. **Pop!**
And Max did a karate chop. **Pop!**

Max and Bob jumped and bounced
and popped away all the worries.

Pop! Pop! Pop!

Now Max doesn't worry half as much as he did.
He hasn't stopped completely
(we all worry, after all — it's natural) . . .

. . . but now, when his head gets too full of worries,
all he has to do is **talk about them,**
and let them float away, one by one.